MALCOM THE MOOSE'S ALASKA VACATION

Malcom the Moose's Alaska Vacation

Published by Gatekeeper Press
2167 Stringtown Rd, Suite 109
Columbus, OH 43123-2989
www.GatekeeperPress.com

Library of Congress Control Number: 2021950585

ISBN (hardcover): 9781662920639
ISBN (paperback): 9781662920646
eISBN: 2021950585

This book is dedicated to all grandparents who cherish
the special moments spent with grandchildren.
To my Granddaughter Bella. I honor the gift of
every moment we spend together. I also dedicate
this book to all of my future grandchildren.

And of course, Malcom loves all the other forest animals like Connie the cougar, Randy the raccoon, and Boris the black bear.

But Malcom's very best friends are Bella and Pa. They visited him every day to rub his nose, pat-pat his horns, and tickle his feet.

But it had been a long, hot summer, and Malcom had not had any good moose food in quite a while. He was feeling a bit tired, ragged and hungry. So, one morning after waking up, Malcom called a taxi.

He took a taxi to the bus stop.

He took
a bus to the
airport.

He took
a plane to
Alaska.

Malcolm was having fun with his friends, but he was getting very full and could hardly eat anymore moose food. Malcolm missed the lodge and all of his friends in Sonora.

So, Malcolm flagged down a taxi. He took a taxi to the bus stop.

He took a bus to the airport.

He took a plane back to Sonora, California.

★ SONORA!

Connie the Cougar

Boris the Blackbear

Bob the Beaver

Randy the Racoon

Millie the Moose

Old Man Elmer the
Bald Eagle

In 2020 when the Covid pandemic took hold, I ended up experiencing some of the life changing events that many others faced. I lost my job, sold my home in Tucson Arizona, and moved in with my daughter's family in Sonora, CA. With lots free time on my hands, I was able to isolate with my new granddaughter Bella.

Part of our daily routine included a walk around the neighborhood and through the parking lot of the Sonora Moose Lodge. We quickly made friends with the large wooden moose on the wall of the Lodge, and named him Malcom. One day on our walk, at the end of a hot summer, Malcom was gone! This created quite the consternation, and Bella was concerned about Malcom. Where was he? Every day we would discuss where he might have gone. After about a week, he was back! They had removed him for maintenance, and he was sanded, painted and refreshed. Bella was very happy to see him again, so we decided he just took a bit of a vacation. He sure looked refreshed and happy upon his return.

This book is a passion project. I enjoy living in the world of imagination with Bella and this story invites readers to join us.

Mack Reagan is an illustrator and comic book artist based in Tucson, Arizona and currently studying in Savannah, Georgia at Savannah College of Art and Design. She enjoys spending her time outside of drawing and painting going on hikes, swimming, exploring nature and hanging out with her dog, Dexter. She loves to use vibrant colors and meaningful brushstrokes in her work and is working to get into the field of concept art and design for animated films and games.

CPSIA information can be obtained
at www.ICGtesting.com
Printed in the USA
BVRC101000260122
627254BV00003B/15